FOR LEO BRANKO AND NIKA SUNAJKO

...AND TO MONIKA AND LUKA IN THE HOPE THEY WILL SOON BREAK THOSE

SEEMINGLY UNBREAKABLE SLEEPING HABITS OF THEIRS.

www.davidmelling.co.uk

HuGLESS DouGLAS AND THE BIG SLEEPoVER

D A V I D   M E L L I N G

Silver Dolphin

Douglas was packing all his things for Rabbit's sleepover. He had a lot of stuff but there was plenty of room at Rabbit's. He packed his honeybee pajamas, a toothbrush, and a storybook.

He was very excited!

"I hope Rabbit reads a bedtime story," thought Douglas as he set off into the woods. His bag was very heavy with all his things. First he got stuck and then he got lost.

He climbed up the nearest tree to see where he was.
Only the tree he chose was quite thin and ...

very...

very...

bendy!

Douglas crashed to the ground and nearly squashed Little Sheep!

"Hello," said Douglas. "I'm going to Rabbit's for a sleepover, but I'm lost."

"I know the way," Little Sheep squeaked.

Douglas smiled. "Why don't you come along too? **THERE'S PLENTY OF ROOM AT RABBIT'S.**"

Douglas scrambled out of the bush and brushed himself off.

"Funny," he thought, "my bag feels even heavier now."

At last they arrived at Rabbit's house.
"Whoo, whoo! You won't fit!" Owl hooted.

"I only brought one little friend,"
said Douglas, "and there's plenty
of room at Rabbit's."

Rabbit's
House

"What about us?" cried the sheep.

Rabbit was very happy to see everyone.
"I love having sheep over for sleepovers," she laughed,
and she waved them all into her house,
one by one by one.

"Your front door does look small," baaed Little Sheep.
"Nonsense!" said Rabbit. "There's plenty of room."

Poor Douglas.

They pushed . . .

and they pulled.

"I don't think this is working," Douglas said.
"Wait a minute!" cried Rabbit, snapping her fingers.
"I'll dig a bigger hole."

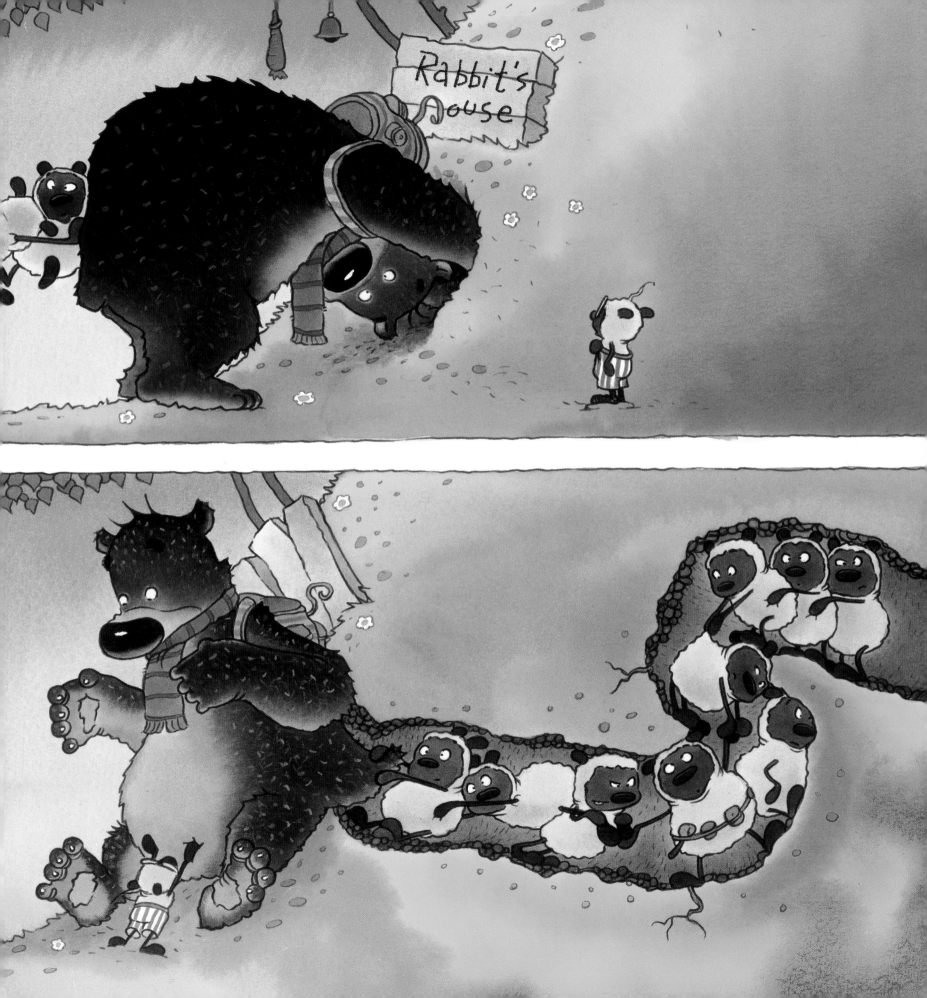

"There now," puffed Rabbit. "Isn't that cozy?"
Douglas wasn't so sure.

"When are you going to read us a bedtime story, Rabbit?" asked Little Sheep.

"As soon as I get in," Rabbit replied. "Snuggle up!"

Everyone shuffled and shifted and squeeeeeeezed about.

"THERE'S NO MORE ROOM AT RABBIT'S!" cried Douglas.

Little Sheep brushed his tickly fleece against Douglas' big round nose.

"AA-AA-AH . . .

Out popped the sheep, one … two … three …

four ... five ... six ... seven ... eight ... nine ... ten!

There were sheep all over the place.

Douglas gathered them together
and looked around.

"There's plenty of room out here," he said.

yawwwwwn!

So Douglas and the sheep settled down and listened
to Rabbit read a story.

"Once upon a time," Rabbit began, "there was a big, big
sleepover . . ."

And, one by one, they all closed their eyes and fell asleep.

What would you pack for a sleepover?

Slippers

Glow-in-the-dark gadgets

Pajamas

Blanket

Storybook

Toothbrush

Woolly socks

Teddy bear

Midnight snacks

Cuddly toy

Headphones

Binky

Robe

Musical alarm clock

Friend

Hugless Douglas and the Big Sleepover
by David Melling

An imprint of Printers Row Publishing Group
A division of Readerlink Distribution Services, LLC
10350 Barnes Canyon Road, Suite 100, San Diego, CA 92121
www.silverdolphinbooks.com

Originally published in Great Britain in 2012
by Hodder Children's Books, a division of Hachette Children's Books
Text and illustrations © 2012 David Melling

Printers Row Publishing Group is a division of Readerlink Distribution Services, LLC.
Silver Dolphin Books is a registered trademark of Readerlink Distribution Services, LLC.

All notations of errors or omissions should be addressed to
Silver Dolphin Books, Editorial Department, at the above address.
All other correspondence (author inquiries, permissions)
concerning the content of this book should be addressed to:
Hachette Children's Group, www.hachettechildrens.co.uk

ISBN: 978-1-68412-376-6

Manufactured, printed, and assembled in China.
First printing, June 2018. WKT/06/18
22 21 20 19 18 1 2 3 4 5